# Dear Parents:

Congratulations! Your child is taking the first steps on an exciting journey. The destination? Independent reading!

**STEP INTO READING®** will help your child get there. The program offers five steps to reading success. Each step includes fun stories and colorful art or photographs. In addition to original fiction and books with favorite characters, there are Step into Reading Non-Fiction Readers, Phonics Readers and Boxed Sets, Sticker Readers, and Comic Readers—a complete literacy program with something to interest every child.

## Learning to Read, Step by Step!

### Ready to Read  Preschool–Kindergarten
• big type and easy words • rhyme and rhythm • picture clues
For children who know the alphabet and are eager to begin reading.

### Reading with Help  Preschool–Grade 1
• basic vocabulary • short sentences • simple stories
For children who recognize familiar words and sound out new words with help.

### Reading on Your Own  Grades 1–3
• engaging characters • easy-to-follow plots • popular topics
For children who are ready to read on their own.

### Reading Paragraphs  Grades 2–3
• challenging vocabulary • short paragraphs • exciting stories
For newly independent readers who read simple sentences with confidence.

### Ready for Chapters  Grades 2–4
• chapters • longer paragraphs • full-color art
For children who want to take the plunge into chapter books but still like colorful pictures.

**STEP INTO READING®** is designed to give every child a successful reading experience. The grade levels are only guides; children will progress through the steps at their own speed, developing confidence in their reading.

Remember, a lifetime love of reading starts with a single step!

© 2015 Viacom International Inc. and Viacom Overseas Holdings C.V. All rights reserved.
Published in the United States by Random House Children's Books, a division of Random House
LLC, 1745 Broadway, New York, NY 10019, and in Canada by Random House of Canada Limited,
Toronto, Penguin Random House Companies. Nickelodeon, Teenage Mutant Ninja Turtles, and
all related titles, logos, and characters are trademarks of Viacom International Inc. and Viacom
Overseas Holdings C.V. Based on characters created by Peter Laird and Kevin Eastman.

Step into Reading, Random House, and the Random House colophon are registered trademarks of
Random House LLC.

Visit us on the Web!
StepIntoReading.com
randomhousekids.com

Educators and librarians, for a variety of teaching tools, visit us at RHTeachersLibrarians.com

ISBN 978-0-553-50866-6 (trade) — ISBN 978-0-553-50867-3 (lib. bdg.)

Printed in the United States of America   10 9 8 7 6 5 4 3 2 1

nickelodeon

# TEENAGE MUTANT NINJA TURTLES™

# Too Much OoZe!

illustrated by Patrick Spaziante

Random House 🏠 New York

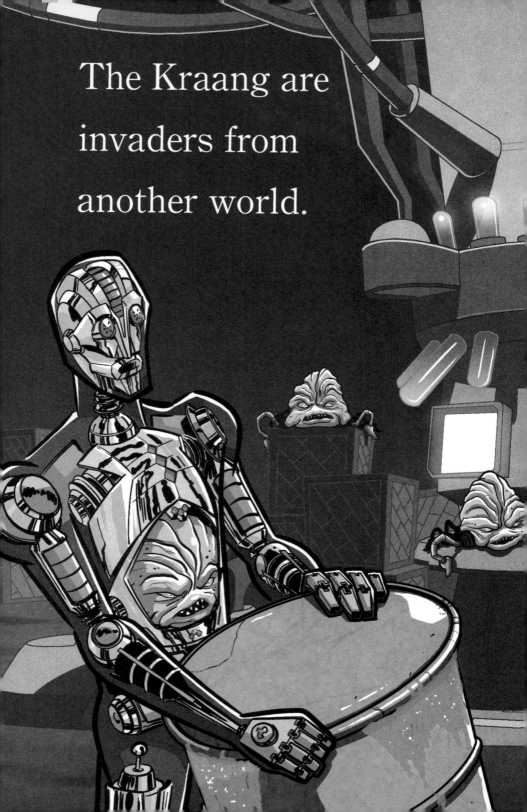

The Kraang are invaders from another world.

They make
a green goo
called mutagen.

Mutagen splashes on
four small turtles.
They grow.

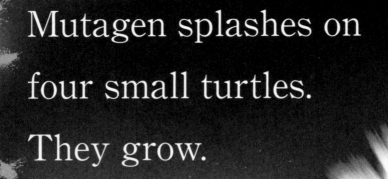

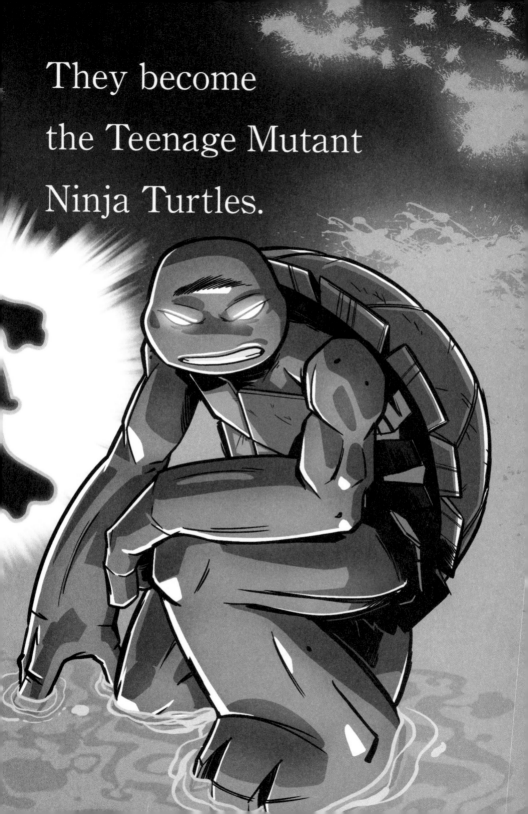

They become
the Teenage Mutant
Ninja Turtles.

Leo, Raph, Donnie,
and Mikey
fight crime.

Shredder is the Turtles' most dangerous enemy.

Shredder is

an evil ninja master.

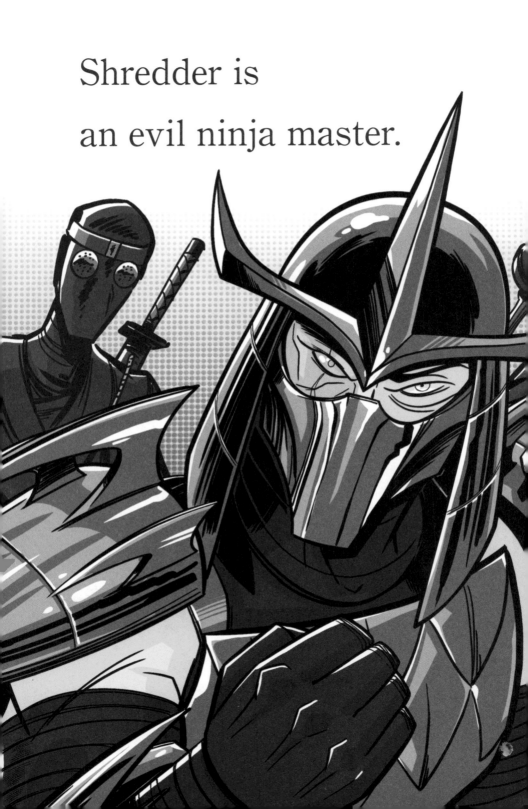

# Many bad guys help him.

Shredder has a plan.
He gets mutagen
from the Kraang.

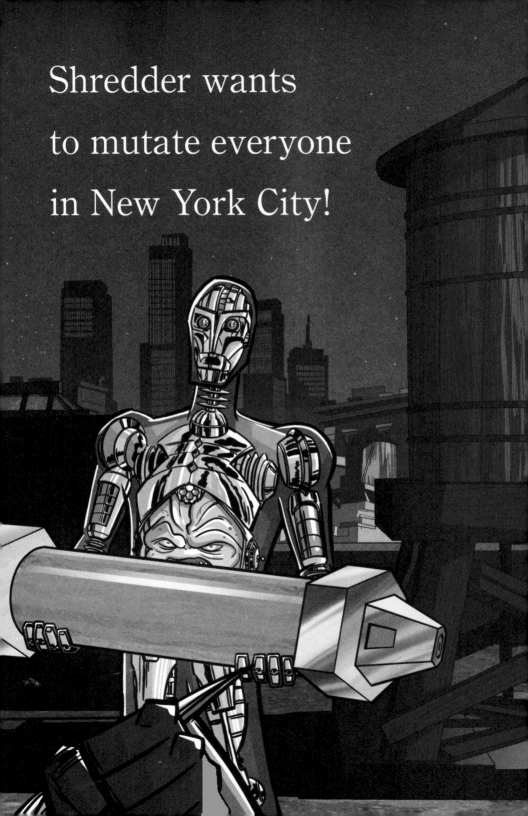

Shredder wants
to mutate everyone
in New York City!

The Turtles must
stop Shredder.

Leo leads
his brothers
into battle!

The bad guys fight
the Turtles.

Mikey kicks.

Raph jumps.

One bad guy
knocks over
the mutagen!

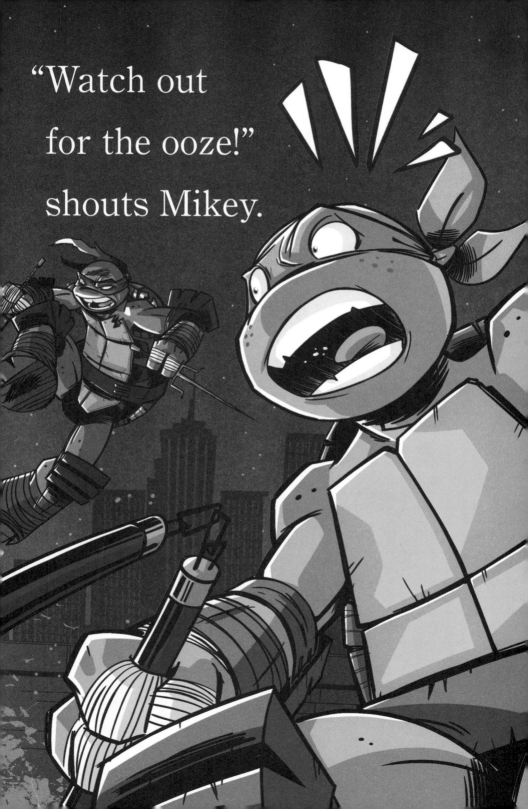

Mutagen splashes on the bad guys.

They change into
mutants named
Dogpound and Fishface!

The Turtles escape.

Shredder's plan is ruined.

The bad guys
will fight the Turtles
another day.

# Turtle Power!

31901062927167